Rick Powell
A BANQUET OF PANECEA

Rick Powell
A BANQUET OF PANACEA

RICK POWELL

WRITER

MARIE HOLDOVAN / JOE MYKUT

EDITORS

MARIE HOLDOVAN

ARTIST

Joseph Mykut -Editor, Cover Images and illustrations

Marie Moldovan - Editor, Publication Layout, and Cover Layout.

A Banquet of Panacea

FOREWARD

I am thrilled to introduce "A Banquet of Panacea," the latest masterpiece from the visionary author, Rick Powell. As his agent, I have had the privilege of witnessing the development of this haunting and thought-provoking story, and I can confidently say that it will leave readers spellbound, disturbed, and questioning where they draw the moral line.

"A Banquet of Panacea" plummets into the darkest recesses of human nature, exploring the unspeakable horrors of child abduction and murder. Rick's unflinching gaze into the abyss of human depravity is counterbalanced by a profound empathy for the victims' families, whose grief and rage are palpable on every page.

But what sets this horror story apart is its bold and unsettling exploration of the concept of closure. When an eccentric billionaire offers the parents of the victims a bizarre and sinister form of retribution—the cannibalization of the serial killer—the narrative takes a dark and unpredictable turn.

With prose that is both lyrical and visceral, Rick Powell masterfully orchestrates a symphony of suspense, horror, and philosophical inquiry. This is a book that will challenge your assumptions about justice, morality, and the human condition.

As an agent, I have had the privilege of working with many

talented authors, but Powell stands out for his fearless commitment to exploring the shadows of human experience. "A Banquet of Panacea" is a triumph of contemporary literature, and I have no doubt that it will leave a lasting impact on readers and the literary world at large.

Working with Rick Powell has been a true collaborative joy. From our initial conversations about the book's premise to the final edits, his dedication to his craft and his willingness to push boundaries has been inspiring. As his agent, it's been my pleasure to support and advocate for his vision, and I'm honored to have played a part in bringing this remarkable story to the world.

~ Joseph Anthony Mykut

of *Cosmic Creation Station*

"Devour the morals of a devious man, and you shall find yourself starved."

~ Marie Moldovan, 2024

"**BREAKING NEWS: WILLIAM SAMUALS RELEASED**

ILLINOIS, MAY 12, 2015 — IN A BIZARRE TURN OF EVENTS, WILLIAM SAMUALS IS FREE TONIGHT, MUCH TO THE OUTRAGE NOT ONLY OF THE RESIDENTS OF THE TOWN OF COOPER'S BLEND BUT ALSO OF THE NATION.

THE TRIAL OF WILLIAM SAMUALS, ALSO KNOWN AS 'BUS DRIVER WILLIE,' TOOK THE MEDIA BY STORM WEEKS AGO WHEN HE WAS ARRESTED FOR THE ABDUCTION, TORTURE, AND MURDER OF SIX CHILDREN IN THAT SOUTH-SIDE TOWN.

THE DEPARTMENT OF JUSTICE HAS INITIATED AN INVESTIGATION INTO THE HANDLING OF EVIDENCE IN THIS CASE, AND THERE ARE EVEN CALLS FOR JUDGE WILKINS TO STEP DOWN.

THE ATTORNEY GENERAL WILL BE ISSUING A TELEVISED STATEMENT WITHIN THE NEXT HOUR REGARDING HOW THE CBPD COULD HAVE GRAVELY MISHANDLED THIS ARREST.

THE PARENTS OF SOME OF THE VICTIMS WERE UNAVAILABLE FOR COMMENT."

"John, are we really doing the right thing?" Meredith asked with nervous apprehension.

She avoided looking at the darkened stage before them; the crimson grand drape that hung down seemed all the heavier in the newly converted theater. Her delicate hand rubbed the freshly lacquered, smooth finish of the large mahogany table where they sat. She tried to conceal how her other hand was on her thigh, clutching the blue fabric of the evening dress she wore.

John placed his hand over hers, feeling the bones through her skin. He remembered how strong and full her hands had been, all those years ago. He tried not to notice how dry, like parchment, they felt now as he answered.

"Honey, it is. We both know it is. We've come too far to turn back now," he said, giving her a feeble smile and wondering if his eyes seemed as heavy as hers, clutching her hand a little tighter for reassurance.

She sighed and straightened up in her seat, but even the soft cushioning of the oak chair could not ease the tension in her shoulders. She looked at the curtained stage fifty feet before them and scanned the arch high above; the bone-white comedy and tragedy masks seemed to scrutinize her and John menacingly. Meredith had tried to delay coming here as much as possible by changing dresses, attempting to conceal some of the silver strands in her red hair, and redoing her makeup, but John saw through it and waited patiently. Despite the two-hour drive, they still managed to be the first ones there.

There was barely any traffic this late in the evening.

She turned her head to look at him. He appeared almost boyish in his black suit, his tie slightly askew as he shifted in his seat. She noticed how he had missed a few spots when shaving; the stubble had a tinge of gray that matched the shade at his temples.

God, she thought, we have both aged so much these last few years.

Where had the time gone?

She swallowed hard, trying not to think about the months that had passed. It still felt just like yesterday.

She sensed he knew what she was thinking.

"Remember that opera we went to years ago? I think it was our first date, and I thought I would try to impress you by being 'cultured'?" he chuckled, shuffling in his seat. "I can't believe that happened."

She gave a weak grin, looking down in recollection.

"You tripped over that man's foot getting to our seats. When you hit the floor, your fart could be heard throughout the whole opera house." She closed her eyes and shook her head.

"And when I got up, I said—"

"I guess the fat lady sang," Meredith cut him off, giggling. She looked at him as he gazed into her eyes. She felt she couldn't have loved him more than at that moment. What he conveyed with that glance communicated more than any words could.

His distraction worked, if only for a little while.

Meredith took a deep breath and looked around. This theater was much smaller than the opera house they had attended years ago. With the absence of a mezzanine or balcony, she guessed this facility could have accommodated about two hundred people at best. It was hard to gauge since the area behind the table where they sat at was void of seating; the evidence of which was erased by the slight sheen of wax on the newly refurbished hardwood floor. When they first entered, her high heels echoed loudly throughout the interior, no matter how lightly she tried to tread.

She figured John must have been reading her thoughts when he said, "It must have cost a small fortune to remodel this. I'm guessing this must have been where the orchestra pit was." He tapped the toe of his dress shoe on the floor, and a slight hollow echo bounced off the Acanthus motif of the freshly papered walls; the brass sconces attached to them seemed to flicker in reply.

John looked at the remaining six seats on the side of the table where they sat; the reddish hue of the oval cushioning almost seemed to stand at attention as they faced the stage. The large table could have seated at least twenty-five people all the way around. "One of those chairs alone is half of our mortgage payment a month," he muttered. "I don't see how—"

The interruption of a door opening far behind them stopped him mid-sentence. Their heads both turned in trepidation toward the sound. Seconds later, a young couple appeared, pausing as they entered and giving John and Meredith a cautious look. The youthful-looking woman's hand clasped onto the forearm of her blond-haired companion in slight fear, while he placed his hand on hers protectively.

They resembled members of a church arriving late to a service, drawing the silent ire of the other attendees with their attire. He was dressed in a white long-sleeved shirt, black tie, and matching pants. She wore a formal white summer dress.

Clutching a small purse to her chest, she tilted her head up to the gentleman who towered over her. Her flaxen hair was tied back in a modest ponytail. John estimated they were about the same age. She waited expectantly for the young man to speak, but he stood there, his jaw clenching in either embarrassment or indecision.

Moments later, John sensed the consternation in the young man and blurted out, "Come on in! The party will start soon!"

Meredith briskly put her hand on his arm. "Dear..." she murmured.

The couple looked at each other. The young man shrugged his shoulders and then motioned with his head for them both to proceed. The close-knit pair hesitantly entered; their footfalls resonating throughout the theater as John gave Meredith an apologetic grin.

The blond-haired man cleared his throat. "Is he here?" he asked faintly.

John was about to make a quip about the obvious but decided against it. "No," he answered, shuffling in his seat. "We just got here a little bit ago ourselves."

The couple looked around the expanse of the theater in silence; their attention diverted to the large, curtained stage.

John stood up and walked toward them, his arm outstretched. "I recognize you from the trial," he said solemnly. "I'm John Richards. You must be Jerry and Ellen Coswell."

The young man looked at the extended hand and shook it reluctantly.

"It's Jeremy," he replied. He swallowed hard and turned to the young girl next to him; she guiltily diverted her eyes as John nodded in her direction.

"...your sister. She was...I mean...I am sorry..." John stammered.

Jeremy pulled the woman close to him.

"Thank you," he interrupted, as he held Ellen close to himself, protectively.

"Sarah...her name was Sarah," his voice grave. "Before our parents died, we promised them we would watch over her."

His dead-eyed stare looked into John's, waiting for a response but hoping not to get one.

"I'm Meredith," John heard his wife say as she came up from behind him, relieved that he did not have to reply. "I am deeply sorry for your loss." She shook both of their hands as Ellen's eyes scrutinized her.

"Your daughter was Janet..." Ellen said softly. "The same age as Sarah."

John looked to Meredith as she answered, "She would have been twelve."

The two women looked at each other with an emotion that John could not define: something resembling pity and defiance.

His wife's eye started to shine from the feeble light with the tear that she was fighting not to let fall.

"She would have been twelve," Meredith repeated.

Their heads all turned in unison to the familiar sound of the door opening behind them, only to be slammed shut loudly by the large figure that entered. The rotund man in a gray business suit strode briskly towards the two couples, the glint from the sweat on his balding forehead matching the spectacles he wore.

"I hope this is not some goddamned joke!" he said, taking a heaving breath. "Is Mr. Zhang here yet?"

The couples looked at each other, at a loss for what to say.

John was in the process of attempting to answer when the portly man looked at the watch on his fat wrist. "I am here right on time at least. I thought I was going to be fucking late. My phone has been ringing off the hook at my office from the goddamn reporters calling. He did say eight o'clock, right?"

Jeremy and John looked at each other with a slight mixture of confusion and embarrassment from the man's entrance.

"Umm... yeah," Jeremy was the first to answer. "That is what he said when he... invited us."

"Invited, my ass. It was more like a direct order, as far as I was concerned," the man blurted out, spittle flying from his lips. "He creeps me out to no end."

"I think that is unanimous here," John added. "I am sorry. I don't believe we have met."

The man extended his hand; his sausage-like fingers gripped John's like a vice as they shook.

"Striener. Lewis Striener. You are Richards, right? I remember you."

John blinked in slight uncertainty, failing to recollect the gentleman before him. "Yes... yes, I am."

He turned to his wife to sort of gauge if she had any memory of the man when Jeremy remarked, "You were in the back of the courtroom shouting when the verdict was read."

"Damn straight! Everyone knew he did it! Everyone! Damn, the police messed it up royally. The missing search warrants, the mishandling of my niece's evidence bag. Those prosecuting attorneys didn't know what they were doing. Idiots!" he barked, pointing a stubby finger at Jeremy, the young man flinching.

Meredith put her hand to her mouth in shocked recollection. "Suzie. Suzie Holmes. She was your niece."

The man's shoulders slumped as he lowered his hand and looked at her, a somber expression coming to his face. "Yeah... yeah. That girl was an angel. What that monster did to our family... what my sister..."

Lewis looked at the four faces staring at him, noticing the shock that was still there from his entrance and outburst.

"I'm... I'm sorry. These last six months since the trial ended and with Sylvia..." His voice trailed off as the red on his craggy face turned from rage to embarrassment.

Ellen walked up to Lewis and put her hand on his forearm. "Please, sit," she said tenderly.

She looked at the others. "Let us all just sit. He should be here any minute."

Lewis looked at her and nodded. They all pulled out the heavy chairs, the feet scraping loudly on the wood floor.

They all seated themselves. John and Meredith sat with the young couple on their right and Lewis on their left, facing the front of the stage in silence. Waiting.

"Is this it?" Jeremy asked in a forlorn voice. "Are we the only ones?"

"I guess so," John answered with a deep sigh.

They all looked at the curtain as it hung motionless; Lewis checked his watch again. "8:05. What the hell?" he whispered. "We have known this guy for almost two years, and he has never been late by a second."

John turned to him. "When did you last hear from Zhang?"

Lewis pulled out the folded letter from his inside jacket pocket, tossing it on the table in front of John. "Probably the same as you all. When I got this in the mail last week."

John unwillingly picked up the paper and opened it, knowing what it might say but reading it anyway:

MR. STRIENER,

AS I COMMUNICATED TO YOU MONTHS AGO, IF THE OUTCOME OF THE TRIAL TOOK THE TURN THAT WE ALL FEARED, I WOULD SEND YOU INSTRUCTIONS ON WHAT I WOULD HAVE TO DO TO TAKE THE NEXT STEP IN DOING WHAT HAS TO BE DONE. THE LEGAL REPRESENTATION I HIRED FOR YOU AND THE OTHER ELEVEN FAMILIES DID WHAT THEY COULD, BUT SADLY, THE CARELESS MISHANDLING OF KEY EVIDENCE AND ARRESTING PROCEDURES IN COOPER'S BLEND COUNTY WAS UNCONSCIONABLE. I HAVE BEEN TAKING THE INITIAL STEPS TO ENSURE THAT JUSTICE WILL BE DONE SINCE IT SEEMS THE LEGAL SYSTEM HAS FAILED, NOT JUST YOU, BUT ALL PARTIES INVOLVED, MISERABLY.

I HAVE CONFIRMATION FROM A FEW OTHER FAMILIES THAT THEY WOULD COMMIT TO PROCEEDING TO THE NEXT LEVEL, AND I HOPE YOU WILL BE JOINING THEM. UNFORTUNATELY, THE OTHERS DECLINED. MY FINAL METHOD TO SET THEIR MINDS AND SPIRITS TO REST WAS SADLY REJECTED, EVEN THOUGH I DID ALL I COULD TO SUPPORT THEM FINANCIALLY AND EMOTIONALLY.

THE TIME AND ADDRESS FOR THE FINAL SOLUTION ARE ATTACHED.

SINCERELY,

MALAKAI ZHANG

P.S.

MY THOUGHTS AND CONDOLENCES GO OUT TO YOU AND YOUR FAMILY DURING THIS TIME. I HAVE ENCLOSED A CHECK FOR ANY FUNERAL EXPENSES FOR YOUR SISTER, SYLVIA. PLEASE USE IT ACCORDINGLY. THE FINAL SOLUTION THAT I HOPE YOU WILL BE ATTENDING WOULD HAVE HEALED HER AND RELIEVED HER OF GRIEF FROM THE LOSS OF HER DAUGHTER, BUT SADLY, SHE CHOSE TO DO OTHERWISE. I AM DEEPLY SORRY.

John folded it closed and handed it back. "It says about the same thing that was sent to Meredith and me."

After a moment, he added, "...your sister... I recall her. I'm..."

Lewis put the paper back in his jacket pocket.

"I know. 'Sorry.' Everyone is 'sorry'! All these words from so many people, but no action," he blurted out, trying to contain his frustration and rage.

"From the lawyers. From other family members. Everyone. Words didn't stop him from going to jail or getting punished. Words did not stop my sister from swallowing a bottle of pills because that man was set free. Oh, no!" Lewis pounded the side of his fist on the table.

Jeremy leaned over the table, looking at him in desperation. "Mr. Striener, I know how you feel. We all do," he said sympathetically. "We have appealed, my sister and I think we have found a lawyer—"

"Bah!" Lewis bellowed, waving him off. "Do you seriously think that will go anywhere?! He was freed! Do your research, kid! I am only a second-rate accountant, but I know a little bit about the legal system. It is done!"

John and Meredith looked at each other during his outburst, both at a loss for what to say to intrude but knowing it wouldn't matter.

Jeremy leaned back in his seat in defeat, shrugging his shoulders as he shook his head at Ellen.

"Once Zhang arrives, I am sure he will be more clear about his 'final solution,' or so he calls it. Let's just wait to see what he has to say," John remarked as he looked from one man to the other, attempting to relieve the tension in the air. "After all, he has done all he can to help us and—"

The muted sound of motors stopped John in mid-sentence as the curtain started to slowly rise, and a beam from an overhead stage lamp came on. The large circle of light illuminated the black trousers and shined shoes of a single individual. The orb of light continued to follow the raising of the curtain to illuminate the chest and other features of a tall, immaculately dressed man, highlighting his bald head and the Asian characteristics of his smiling face.

"You are correct, Mr. Richards," his voice resonated around the theater. "All of your questions will be answered, and I have been here for quite some time."

***

The silence was deafening as he stood there. He raised his hands together before his chest, the fingertips barely touching as he acknowledged them with an appreciative nod.

"Okay, Zhang. What gives?" Lewis asked as he stood up, pushing the chair behind him.

The frustration in his voice was evident as he continued, not giving the imposing figure on the stage a chance to answer. "The news better be good. Bringing us all out here to God knows where. Cryptic letters. Not hearing from you these last few months."

Lewis took a step forward, his voice rising. "You better be here to tell us that you used all these mysterious riches you have to hire a hitman to blow Samuals' brains out! Do you have any idea the nightmare..."

"Sit down, Mr. Striener!" the tall man ordered; his commanding voice echoed. His posture and pose did not change as he glared at the large man. His dark eyes seemed to glint from the beam of the lamp that reflected off them.

Lewis' heavily jowled mouth shut, and he slowly sat back down in his chair, his contained anger still radiating from his face.

"Thank you," Zhang said, clearing his throat. "I am glad you few were able to make it. Believe me, it was no easy undertaking to prepare for an event such as this. When the verdict was read, I immediately had to get the preparations underway for you all."

"Prepare? For what?" Ellen asked, trying to make her voice sound less nervous than she actually was.

Mr. Zhang clapped his hands twice rapidly; the piercing sound made Ellen flinch in her seat.

The faint sound of stomping heeled shoes could be heard, getting louder and louder, as a multitude of figures of the same nationality as Zhang materialized from the opposite sides of the stage; silent, stone-faced figures dressed in waiter and waitress attire, their maroon vests and ties matching the color of the velvet-lined walls.

They all carried plates of fine china, polished silverware, cloth napkins, and assorted cutlery and proceeded to make place settings in front of the attendees at the table; their emotionless faces saying not a word to the confused looks of the five that were seated.

"What the hell?" John muttered to his wife as he sat there frozen, watching the rapid motion of the servers make neat, professional settings in front of him. They seemed almost choreographed as if they had done this numerous times.

In between the tinkling sound of various-sized pieces of silverware being placed on the table, Lewis' voice could be heard in disbelief. "What the hell is this? Some sort of dinner for the defeated?"

"Not quite," Zhang replied. His accent was distinguishable as he spoke steadily, gazing at the five as they looked at each other. "Of course, this feast could be open to more than one interpretation. It is a 'victory dinner' of sorts to you. A 'last meal' to others." He clasped his hands in front of his face, the two forefingers pointed upward and tapping his lips with a slight smirk.

John held his hand up to halt when he saw Lewis was about to voice his disgust once again.

"Mr. Zhang," John said, trying to contain his composure. "I am sure I speak for everyone here when I say that we appreciate all that you have done for us, but you have been an enigma ever since you entered our lives."

"With the disastrous outcome of Samuals' release, we are in dire need of answers and want this nightmare to be over. We need to get on with our lives," he continued, clenching his jaw in vexation. "We wanted—no, needed—him to pay. We are at a loss for what to do, so excuse our frustration."

John took his wife's hand as she looked at him with a mixture of pride and sorrow. "We are angry, and we are tired of all of it."

"Do you remember the day we first met?" Zhang asked as he clasped his hands behind his back and started to slowly pace the stage.

"I... I think so," John answered, looking weakly at the others. Zhang nodded at him, urging him to continue.

"I remember the days before the trial. You came to our house," John looked up at the shadows of the ceiling, far beyond the glare of the lamp, recollecting. "We were afraid that we would have to take out a second mortgage on our house. I hadn't worked in months. Meredith and I were... lost."

Jeremy saw the despair in his face and tried to interrupt John's memory.

"You approached us as my sister and I were sitting in the car in the parking lot at the police station when we got the news that they found Sarah," he addressed Zhang. "We couldn't find the strength to get out of the car until after you talked to us."

Zhang nodded appreciatively. He then turned to Lewis with a tilt of his bald head, his domineering look anticipating what the man would say.

Lewis sat back in his seat with an irritated sigh.

"You came to my office, introduced yourself, and gave me your business card. You didn't say much except your offer to help," he said, regarding Zhang with disdain for the way the man stood there, scrutinizing him. "Then again," He added, "you knew that you wouldn't have to explain much. I bet you knew I would find some things out on my own."

Just then, two more waiters appeared. One with a tray of wine glasses and the other with a finely carved silver bucket with the necks of open bottles protruding from it. One waiter placed the glasses in front of the five while the other poured with robotic synchronicity.

John caught a glimpse of the label and gasped in shock. "Whoa! Wait... is that...?" he asked, his wife giving him a quizzical expression.

Lewis snatched one of the bottles from the bucket and read the label; an ingratiating smile appeared on his face. "'Domaine de la Romanée-

Conti,'" he announced, shoving the bottle back into the bucket harshly, clinking them against the others. "Then again, we wouldn't expect anything less, would we?"

Zhang rocked on the heels of his shoes for a moment, with his hands behind his back, the two men looking at each other as if in a game of mental chess.

Ellen blinked at the glass of wine before her, afraid to touch it as she asked, "What is going on? What 'things' did you find out?"

Lewis took a deep breath, his gaze not leaving the imposing figure on the stage.

"Mr. Ching Ho Zhang, also known as Malakai, was born in the Guangdong province of Guangzhou, China, in 1945. Born to the parents of migrant workers who died in 1961 (due to unsavory conditions, no doubt), he was shuffled around to numerous orphanages (which probably had the same, if not worse, conditions during Chairman Mao's rule at that time)."

Zhang looked at him with a grin, his eyes not leaving Mr. Striener's face as he waited for the large man to continue.

Lewis picked up his glass, took a long sip, and inspected the contents appreciatively in the theater light; the others gazing at him with intense interest as he recommenced Zhang's biographical history.

"He disappeared off the grid until 1972 when he showed up as a family member of Deng Xiaoping, the most powerful figure in the People's Republic of China.

Zhang graduated from Peking University in 1977, right around Mao's death, receiving top honors in History, World Economics, and such. He moved to America in the '80s, right after the Tiananmen Square debacle. There were rumors and conjecture about his involvement in that, and in the late '70s when his dear ol' adoptive daddy 'destroyed his opponents' after Mao kicked the bucket.

Fast forward to the 1990s when Zhang changed his name and studied existentialism (for reasons I have not a clue), traveled to Tibet a few times, came back to America, and made millions in the stock market until the 9/11 event. The impending recession did not seem to affect him in the slightest.

In 2007, Zhang could be seen hanging around Li Ka-shing, Warren Buffet, and the like. He started becoming a sort of philanthropist, doing a great deal of charitable work, and was even involved in the development of the Tsz Shan Monastery, an institute of Chinese Buddhist practice and spiritual education. There were whispers that he helped Li donate $1.7 billion for that."

A slight whistle could be heard from John as he picked up his glass and carefully took a sip, his eyes widening at the taste of the wine.

Lewis turned to John. "Yeah," he nodded towards the glass. "Our 'mysterious benefactor' has made it a habit of helping people, not those of the famous elite, mind you, for the last few years, showing up in cases like ours."

"What? What do you mean?" Jeremy asked.

Lewis rolled the stem of the wine glass, admiring the liquid. "Have you ever heard about the Reinholt case?"

"God," Meredith exclaimed.

"Those people that were murdered in that restaurant. Of course, it was all over the news." Meridith turned her head away, momentarily regretting what she said, recollecting how their daughter's picture was all over the media outlets, and the internet...

Zhang stood frozen on the stage; his eyes still unblinking from the beam of light that shone off them.

"Yep," Lewis remarked. "One of my so-called 'informants' showed me a picture after the trial. You could see Zhang in the background talking to one of the families. Then another picture of him talking to another family."

"Wow, Mr. Striener," Jeremy remarked. "Are you sure you're a CPA? You would make a great detective."

Lewis chuckled. "Kid, trying to keep my business running in this economy, I research a lot of stuff. Hell, who needs to pay an accountant today when you can do your taxes online for free?"

He continued, "I especially do my homework when someone approaches me to help me financially. That is something we all have in common here," Lewis looked at Zhang up on the stage. "But then again, you already knew we would not turn you away, didn't you?"

They all turned to Zhang, gauging his response. There was silence for a few moments until the tall Asian man unclasped his hands behind his back and proceeded to clap in an apathetic form of applause.

"Very well done, Mr. Striener," he responded. "I commend you on the probing of my biographical history. Of course, it is, how do you say... 'skimming the surface' of my less-than-illustrious background."

Lewis raised his glass in a meager toast. "Oh, I am sure there is more. Much more, but I fear digging any deeper would be detrimental to my well-being."

Zhang nodded, respectively. "You found what I wanted you to find, Mr. Striener. As for your well-being, I would never harm you for anything you would uncover but instead bring comfort to the tragedy that has befallen your life."

He addressed the rest of them, "All your lives. When you leave here tonight, rest assured that your life will be enriched in ways you cannot imagine, and the much-needed healing process will begin."

Meredith lifted her glass in a weak hand, shakily putting it to her lips, taking a scant sip and not tasting it. "That will not get our daughter back," she muttered, trying to hold back her tears. "That monster is free. No amount of money will ever get her back." She set the glass down, almost spilling it.

John turned to his wife. The look on her face matched the helplessness he felt. They had tried so hard to get through the last few months, and no amount of counseling, spiritual help, or love could ever convalesce from losing their daughter in such a way. He knew he had always been her anchor in all the years they had been married, but the deterioration this had caused was something he could not control.

John pushed his chair back and stood up. "Look, Mr. Zhang," he said, still looking at his wife. "I am sure I speak for everyone here when I say that there is no way we can thank you enough for all you have done."

"I do not care about your reasons for doing this or your history," he turned and gazed indifferently at the man on the stage. "But whatever you have planned here will not change anything. We are beyond any Tony Robbins-Suze Orman crap now."

"Yeah," Lewis blurted out. "Unless you are here to tell us that you put a bullet in the head of Samuals, then I agree." He took another gulp of wine and pushed his chair back to stand up.

Jeremy and Helen looked at each other with a shrug of their shoulders and proceeded to do the same.

"Rest assured, my friends. Before this night is through, Mr. Samuals will be taken care of, and you will leave here with a renewed sense of life," Zhang's emotionless, haunting voice seemed to echo all around.

"Please stay." A sardonic smile formed on his face that reflected the light, almost glimmering as the five froze in place.

They then heard the rolling of wheels and the sound of switches as other lamps blazed from overhead; bathing Zhang as other waiters and waitresses appeared from both sides of the stage. Several were wheeling out an enormous stainless-steel grill as others pulled out a small, cloth-covered table; an array of different-sized surgical instruments reflected the gleam of the elevated lights.

Zhang was oblivious to the servants behind him as he motioned to the confused and shocked looks of the small group before him; his outstretched arm with his palm up in the direction of the table that they were about to vacate.

"Please," Zhang said hauntingly.

They exchanged looks with each other; a mixture of shock and confusion in more than a few furrowed brows at what he said. As they seated themselves again, Ellen was the first to ask, "What do you mean by 'taken care of'?"

In between the sounds of the servants wheeling out a few other smaller tables—covered, but with the unmistakable sounds of china and the tinkling of unseen metal implements—Zhang replied, "My dear, there is one thing you all have in common here tonight, and that is that justice has not been served. Tonight, will answer all your questions and rectify that situation."

Their attention was diverted by a humming sound as a large steel hood descended from the track lighting above the stage. It lowered directly above the positioned grill; a wide, flexible foiled duct, attached to something higher than they could see, elongated as it dropped. Other waiters were pulling out gas lines from the ends of the stage to attach to the grill while the guests watched.

"You are about to witness and take part in a ritual that few have ever experienced. The likes of which will change you for years to come," Zhang announced.

A waiter appeared at his side with a serving tray and a glass of wine. Zhang took it and raised it before him."Gānbēi," he said. "A toast to you all, and may you not just dine well in body, but may you dine well in spirit!"

He waited until they raised their glasses—a mixture of apathy and discontent on their faces. They all took a long drink; Jeremy and Ellen took another, longer sip, a slight marveling on their faces from the extravagant flavor of the wine.

The squeaking of wheels from the right of the stage could be heard as a hospital gurney is slowly pushed by a stone-faced waitress; the shape of a body unmistakable from the white sheet that covered it.

Ellen let out a slight shriek as Meredith gasped. What shocked them more than the sudden appearance of such a thing was something else:

The covered body struggled, and muffled sounds could be heard as the sheet twitched.

"Wait a goddamn minute!" Lewis shouted. "What the hell is this?!?!"

John said not a word as he gaped, open-mouthed, to the scene before him.

The shrill noise of the wheels ceased as the waitress stopped the gurney next to Zhang and proceeded to unroll the sheet off of the squirming body underneath; the tall Asian man finishing his long drink of wine in a satisfied manner and showing no concern for the other's sounds of disgust.

Clad only in a pair of boxers—damp with sweat from his exertions—a middle-aged man lay bare on the gurney's frame.

Thick, leather belts chafed the man's shins and wrists, holding him firmly in place. A broader strap crossed his hairy, perspiring belly, so tight it seemed to nearly slice into his abdomen's skin.

His grayish hair was a wild mess, the result of frantic headshaking in a futile attempt to dislodge the duct tape sealing his mouth.

Raising his head, the man tried to shout through the adhesive barrier, eyes bulging with a hateful glare directed at Zhang.

"Dear... God," Jeremy muttered in shock.

Meredith stood up abruptly, her hands to her mouth, her chair tipping over onto the polished floor. The sound of the oak wood hitting was the only other sound as tears started to well up in her eyes on her pale face.

"Whoa, whoa. Hold on," John said as he wrapped his arm around his shocked wife, pulling her close. His other arm extended, palm forward, as if trying to halt the scene before him. "Just... just wait one minute here!"

"I knew it!" Lewis leaned back in his chair, shocked.

"I had a feeling that's what this was all about," he said resignedly, with a mixture of loathing and hate, as he slowly leaned forward.

"So, this is it. Your 'final solution'? You're going to kill the fucker, and we're going to celebrate with dinner?!?!" Lewis swallowed hard after saying the last words, trying to contain the bile that was starting to rise in his throat.

Zhang gave an indifferent shake of his head. "Not really. You see... he IS going to be the dinner."

The ensuing silence was shattered by a loud clicking that echoed around the theater—a sound they soon recognized as bolts sliding into place, locking the heavy doors.

Ellen screamed, "WHAT IS GOING ON?!"

"ZHANG! YOU CANNOT BE SERIOUS!" Lewis shouted as he stood and pounded his fist on the table, making the utensils bounce with a clatter barely audible over Meredith's sobs; her hands covering her face as she cried into John's shoulder.

Jeremy took Ellen's hand, pulled her out of her seat, and they rushed toward the entrance from which they had come.

"Lewis was right!" John shouted, holding his weeping wife close. "This has to be some sort of sadistic joke!"

They heard a shout and a curse from Jeremy far behind them as a waiter approached Zhang, taking the empty wine glass held out to him and exiting to the right of the stage. "Not a joke at all, Mr. Richards. Have you ever known me to jest about anything?"

"But what you are suggesting is sick! Barbaric! After all my wife and I have been through, after everything we and the other families have endured! To shock us with this and to bring that monster here, expecting us to...?!" John bellowed, his face red with rage and disgust, trying to avoid looking at the struggling man bound to the gurney, wriggling violently to free himself.

"What exactly did you expect when I invited you all here?" Zhang asked in an authoritative voice. He walked stoically across the stage, his arms spread out, admiring the recesses above him. "Something as grand as this was provided for you. Did you expect life-altering words on how to cope with the unspeakable loss you all have suffered? Some sort of monetary compensation for how your mockery of a legal system has failed you?"

Jeremy materialized next to John, Ellen's hand clasped in his, a visage of fright on his face. "We are locked in here!" he blurted out. He turned to his sister. "Call the police!"

"You are more than free to do so," the tall man said, cocking his head and scrutinizing Ellen as she shakily dug into her purse. "But what exactly would you tell them? Are you sure you would want your names and faces in the media more than they already have been?"

Ellen ignored him, tapping on her phone frantically.

"WAIT!" Lewis shouted at her.

She froze and looked at him with tear-filled eyes, one shaking finger poised above the screen.

Lewis, with his hands planted firmly on the table, glared at her. "Just hold on a second!" he said through gritted teeth, his red, perspiring face struggling to regain control.

Ellen and Jeremy both looked at John as he stared at Zhang incredulously, indecisive about what to do.

Jeremy was about to protest when John held up his hand.

"Yeah... just... just," he muttered. Meredith whipped her head back to look at him, wide-eyed and shocked, her face smeared from the tear-streaked mascara.

"Zhang... Malakai... whoever you are," he continued, ignoring the look from his wife. "What makes you think that we could even... listen... just let us out. We won't say a thing to anyone. We promise."

"Oh, I am not worried about that, Mr. Richards," Zhang assured him. "When this night is through, I have complete confidence that it will be the furthest thing from your mind."

Samuals began to thrash violently on the gurney, causing the unlocked wheels to roll feebly around on the stage. Emotionless waiters appeared and locked the wheels, stopping the motion. They disappeared just as quickly.

"Now, let me ask you all a question," Zhang posed, his voice steady and commanding. "What DID you expect the reason to be for why I called you here tonight? What did you secretly hope for? News that I had killed Samuals? That I got him 'whacked,' as you Westerners are fond of saying?"

No one said a word as they looked at him in shock. Their silence was the answer he expected.

Meredith looked at Samuals with a mixture of disgust and fear. She glared at Zhang. "This?! This is what you intended to do all this time?" she asked in a raspy, dry voice.

"Mr. Striener, a question for you," Zhang asked with a degree of confidence, ignoring Meredith. "You have spoken to other victims' families that I have assisted in the past, am I correct?"

Lewis straightened up and, after moments of contemplative silence, replied, "Yes, I have."

"Did they reveal to you my 'outré' method and the details of how I assisted them?" Zhang inquired.

Lewis thought for a moment, then bowed his head as if defeated. He then looked up into the recesses of the high-ceilinged theater, an odd look on his face. "No, they didn't. They just said what you did... helped them 'in ways they could not imagine.' You helped them move on and..."

There was a sound of a slight whoosh as the flames of the gas grill came to life, lit by a few waiters. Two large cooks appeared from the left of the stage, men of the same nationality as the rest, with countenances void of any emotion. They pushed out a cart identical to the others except for the items that lay upon it: an assortment of stainless steel, battery-operated reciprocating saws, their unused blades shining from the lights above.

The others took no notice of this as they were looking intently at Mr. Striener, enthralled by the realization on his face and waiting for him to finish.

"Go on, Mr. Striener," Zhang said authoritatively. "You were saying?"

Lewis looked to the others, then to Zhang. "They seemed at peace."

"...dear God..." Ellen muttered as she fell to her seat.

"No God, young lady," Zhang said. "Just a method of revenge achieved in ways only conducted by a few individuals throughout the world. Ways not spoken of except in whispers."

Zhang strode to the form of Samuals, who was thrashing less and less as his tense muscles weakened.

"But... this?! This... is—" Jeremy started to say as he sat down, pulling his sister to him.

"The only way, Mr. Coswell!" Zhang snapped, turning towards him. "Rest assured, if you do not go through with this, I will unlock those doors, and you can be free to go. All of you. Even the man who has done all of this to you!"

"NO!" Meredith screamed, making John flinch. "THAT MONSTER CANNOT GO FREE!" She began to sob and wrapped her arms around her stomach. "My baby! What he did to my... my little..." She wailed as she sat down heavily.

John slumped, at a loss for what to do, sitting down to console his wife. "Damn you!" he said through gritted teeth. "You are not just doing this for us. You are getting a sick, sadistic joy out of this, aren't you?"

Zhang's eyes narrowed as he looked at John, a slight smirk on his face. "I would be lying if I said that I do not get a semblance of pleasure from my methods. After all, a person's life's work should be enjoyable, should it not?"

"As for those of you who have come here tonight," he continued, "there is something that I have seen in each one of you during the trial and the events leading up to it. I have seen it in your eyes at certain times when you looked at him. It is something I have seen in others in the past. It is something I have seen in my reflection throughout my life."

His voice was so hypnotic and commanding they did not even notice the chefs vigorously washing the exposed parts of Samuals as he gave a few feeble thrashes, as if cleaning a prime cut of meat.

"Hunger. A hunger for revenge."

"...no..." John muttered, shaking his head weakly.

Zhang raised his voice. "I have seen many things throughout my life, Mr. Richards," he shouted. "I watched my parents die when our government let us down. Are you familiar with the Great Chinese Famine? Fifteen million died. We had to do what we could to survive."

Zhang paused before continuing, his voice filled with intensity. "I learned at a young age, an incredibly young age, that self-preservation is the most basic of animal instincts, and any that stand in the way of that shall be—"

The sound of one of the chefs turning on one of the reciprocating saws brought a whine to life behind Zhang.

"-destroyed."

"...no, please...," Meredith pleaded, in a frail whisper.

"Your society has been weak. Very weak for an exceedingly long time..."

Ellen swallowed hard, her eyes wide and unblinking as she stared at Samuals; she realized she felt nothing as his eyes bore into hers, silently weeping.

"-and I have spent the last 30 years of my life successfully causing, what you might say 'ripples', in the sea of injustice that will eventually lead to a tide of retribution for any that will harm a child, as I have seen so many in our country suffer. I have created a plan-"

The other chef uncovered one of the small tables that was rolled out; an assortment of glass spice bottles caught the light from overhead.

"-that is twofold. A therapeutic means that will avenge those innocent lives and bring new enlightenment to the other lives that were shattered. This is a once-in-a-lifetime experience-"

Lewis slapped his hand over his mouth as one of the chefs pushed the spice cart next to the grill. The chef opened a couple of random bottles, set them back, and then headed to the other cart. Carefully, the chef lifted a scalpel from the cart.

Both chefs walked to the gurney. The shrill of the saw failed to drown out Zhang's voice, which grew louder in tone.

-, an experience that will show you that revenge is not a 'dish best served cold'-"

"...this is not the way..." Jeremy muttered. He knew he should protest with more conviction than that, but

Zhang's voice was hypnotic as hypnotic as what was about to occur before his very eyes. He thought for a split second that this was wrong. So very, very wrong but their sister...the other's daughters...

What Samuals had done to them? Jeremy wanted him to pay.

Samuals had a burst of energy—just for a moment—in one last feeble attempt to get free.

Jeremy pulled his gaze away from Samuals to look at the group seated around the table.

They all had a look of extreme disgust mixed with expectation.

At that moment, he knew they all wanted it. Some primal instinct to see Samuals suffer. To see Samuals in pain. That deep down, they all wanted this. Waited for this on a deep psychological level.

"- but served medium rare and properly seasoned!" Zhang continues.

Jeremy whipped his head back to the chefs as they walked behind the gurney, scalpel, and saw poised above the twitching thigh of Samuals.

Jeremy tried to will himself to stand but could only slam his hands onto the table; his palms clammy with sweat as he shouted, "Do it!"

The chef lowered the saw blade onto Samual's thigh, immediately cutting into the tense muscle as blood sprayed onto his chef's coat. The muffled scream from Samuals could faintly be heard through the gag as he shrieked. The thrashing of his body just made the jagged blade go deeper as Zhang stepped to the side so they all could watch.

Ellen jumped in her seat; a quick scream was issued from her lips. It echoed around the theatre as she let out another. This one almost resembles that of joy.

Meredith turned away, burying her head in John's shoulder. Her hand clutched his jacket's lapel, trembling, as a shriek escaped her lips. John's eyes remained fixed on the horrific scene—the carving of the first large piece of flesh from Samuals thigh. His knee and foot twitched involuntarily, a visceral response to the excruciating pain.

Beside them, Lewis emitted a muffled sound, his hand still covering his mouth, his eyes wide with disbelief and shock.

Meanwhile, the chef handled the bloody, dripping flesh with a grotesque sense of care, carrying it to the grill. The air shimmered with heat as he seasoned the meat with an array of spices and flung it onto the grill, eliciting a sizzling hiss.

An unseen fan whirred to life, and the makeshift flue attached to the vent above the grill vibrated, struggling to vacuum the smoke from the charring flesh. Yet, it did little to mitigate the acrid stench of the meat as it cooked.

The chef with the saw wasted no time starting on the other thigh. Streams of blood poured and pumped from the cavity of the first thigh, drenching the emotionless cook; the whir of the saw matched the rhythm of the blood splattering onto the floor.

Samual's eyes were white, the irises and pupils rolled up into his head as the gag turned crimson, stained from biting down on his cheek or other parts of his mouth. His twitching leg forced the saw deeper, hitting bone with a resonating crunch.

Dear God, we cannot go through with this, were the thoughts racing through John's head. He became aware that Meredith was now watching the nightmarish scene on the stage, and for a moment, her hitching and trembling seemed off somehow.

He became vaguely aware of Zhang's voice, continuing in the same commanding, monotonous drone: "...in the 19th century, it was not unusual for Chinese executioners to eat the heart and brains of the criminals..."

(Another piece gets tossed on the grill. The hiss. The smell. John sees the former piece turned over—a pair of tongs in a large hairy fist. A glimpse of the underside of that piece charred; the grill lines perfect, as if on a prime cut of sirloin.)

Lewis's stomach churned with disgust—or was it hunger? —as he tried to will himself to stand but could not. Had the lights dimmed, or was he on the verge of passing out? He couldn't tell. He heard Zhang's voice as the chefs meticulously started on Samual's calf.

"...people used humans not only for food and medicine but also expressed their feelings of hatred or revenge by publicly eating the flesh and bones of their fellow men..."

Time seemed to slow down for Ellen as she let out one loud, audible sob; the movement on the stage before her blurred as she mouthed one word: "...Sarah..."

"...so, you see, this is the final, and ultimate solution? Your laws, your lawyers, your courts, and even your government have failed you. The disgust you believe you see here is nothing compared to what my culture, and others, have witnessed throughout the centuries..." Zhang continued.

The blood that covered the stage had turned into a small stream. It began to flow towards them, drawing Jeremy's attention. Captivated by the movements reflected on the red, liquid surface, Jeremy watched as the men methodically continued to carve at the twitching body on the table. Their silhouettes worked with robotic precision, casting shadows that danced eerily in the light.

"This cannot be happening..." Jeremy whispered.

(A sizzle could be heard as another piece is tossed on the grill.)

"...you will feast not just of body, but of mind. Nothing in all the world compares to the first taste of the individual who has taken the life of a loved one. Especially that of a child, the most horrific of all crimes..."

They did not notice the lithe, pale hands of the waiters and waitresses coming up behind them, putting cloth bibs in place of dress and shirt collars; mechanically tucking them in and adjusting them in place.

"...sometimes it does not take much to change someone's palate. Be it in their mind or the taste buds in their tongue..."

(The grill was half-filled in such a short period. A few shorter chefs appeared to take over the cooking process while the two larger ones kept up with the meticulous cutting of the unrecognizable form on the gurney; the bones and cartilage of both legs gleamed in the shining lamps overhead.)

John looked at the rictus-like face of the man who murdered their daughter. The teeth that were exposed and biting down on the gag were now covered with a pinkish hue as he foamed at the mouth in his death throes.

Strips of flesh fell to the stage with an audible slap. John could not imagine the unnameable suffering the murderer was experiencing, but he realized one thing:

The smile that came to his face.

"...changing a society can be done in much the same way. Instead of a sprinkle of spices, you take a sprinkle of individuals. A select few who can..."

Meredith turned her face up to her husband as he held her tightly to him. Their eyes locked for a split second before their heads almost turned in unison to the activity on stage—a vision of white chef coats covered in crimson, moving to-and-fro to the sound of shoes walking in blood, like a moist symphony echoing in such a place as this.

That split-second look they gave each other said more than words could ever have said. It would not be understood until later why John felt that Meredith's hitching sobs from moments ago seemed off somehow:

Those sobs were distorted giggling.

(The sizzle and stench were intoxicating...as intoxicating as the tall Asian man on stage as he walked slowly to the dying meal that was once William Samuals. One arm, void of flesh and muscle except for the hand attached to it, swung free from the gurney as one chef unbuckled the strap holding it down; a rivulet of blood poured down at Zhang's feet as he approached. The chef, concentrating on a sweated brow, started cutting into the bulbous side of the ribcage with a smaller battery-operated saw.)

"His...heart," Lewis said with a gag. "Just...just stab him in the...heart." He did not know where those words came from. Somewhere deep down in his subconscious, deep down as he sat, in disbelief of how the body (mostly resembling a torso now) could still be breathing! For some unknown reason, the images that flashed through his head were instances of the past. Times when he and his sister used to play Monopoly in their old apartment when they were kids...him holding his niece for the first time, the look on Sylvia's face as he held the small bundle...other times...

What other memories could there have been, but that bastard...that filth!

"His heart, Mr. Streiner?" Zhang replied with a smirk. "No. We have to save that-"

A waitress walked up the few steps to the stage, a wide, gleaming silver platter in her hands. The chef flipped over a few pieces of the meat; their juices dripped into the flames of the grill (like the sweat from his wide forehead); making an even louder sizzling noise as Zhang continued.

"- for what is an exquisite meal without a decadent dessert!"

With tongs and fork in hand, the chef started putting the charred pieces on the tray; each one dripping with a myriad of juices that became a puddle on the immaculate silver finish. When the tray had an abundance of steaming meat, the waitress turned and stepped off the stage, walking carefully towards the seated five.

They watched as the woman, joined by a waiter, neared them. A cloth towel was draped over his forearm in the most stoic of manners. In his hand at his side was a pair of tongs that matched the ones used by the chef on the stage.

The chef was now scraping the grill with a wire brush, preparing it for the larger pieces that were cut off of Samuals. The sound of the piercing whine as the saw cut into the ribcage filled the air.

They watched with a mixture of horror and fascination as the pair walked in front of the table; the woman extending out the tray as the waiter delicately transferred a piece to each of their plates.

Ellen heard a dull wet thud under her chair as she stared at the chunk of meat that was placed before her. She realized it was her cell phone that fell into the puddle of blood under her seat; having fallen from her limp hand as her arms hung numb at the sides of the chair.

"This is...how can we...I can't..." She muttered to herself.

"My friends," Zhang proclaimed. "You have been given a once-in-a-lifetime opportunity. A chance to enact the ultimate in retribution. To show you a symbol of good faith, and to leave the final option up to you-"

The sounds of all the unseen doors in the theater unclicking echoed all around them as they sat oblivious to the sound; their unblinking eyes glued to the fine white china plates and the steaming meat laid out in the congealing liquid that was slowly forming.

"-you can stay here and be free or leave and forever remain a prisoner. A prisoner of doubt, not knowing what true justice is!"

The cooks and staff all paused in their labors as they stared, unblinking at the seated five. They were waiting as five pairs of eyes gazed, hypnotic-like, at the meal before them.

1 1/2 years later:

The woman dabbed her eyes again with the Kleenex, which was now just a wadded-up damp ball from crying the last hour.

She sat on the bench outside the police station. The crisp winter air had a scatter of flakes that the weatherman predicted would be six inches of snow by morning. She did not feel the chill as she watched individuals walk up the concrete steps to get to the warmth of the station.

Some of them, she guessed, were newspaper and television reporters in a hurry to get the story.

She wanted to go in. Needed to go in, but she did not have the strength. It took everything she had just to get in the car to get there. Ron was passed out on the couch from last night's bender, and she just wanted to take that half-drunk bottle of Jack from his hand and join her husband in intoxicated oblivion.

She couldn't. She wanted to, but she couldn't. She knew when they called about the arrest, they both needed to be there, but she was scared to death. She waited for the news to show his picture. To see what he looked like before she drove there. She flicked the TV from one station to the next so she could prepare herself first.

She knew right then and there that he was the right man. Something in her gut told her so.

Davey was just 9.

They did not even have him for 10 years. Not even a decade before a monster resembling a man did what he did. There was even talk about more boys. This never happened in this town. Never.

After taking the hottest shower imaginable and driving for forty-five minutes to get there, having not left the house in about a week, she found herself unable to muster the energy to go through those doors.

She looked down at the cracked concrete beneath her feet, shivering—and it wasn't from the slow drop in temperature.

She should have waited for Ron to wake up. She can't cry again. How many tears can a person shed?

"Mrs. Wallace?" a voice interrupted her thoughts as she wiped her swelling eyes.

She looked up to see a man in a full-length wool topcoat, sprinkled with flakes, giving her a kind look. His well-groomed brown hair had greyish streaks that matched his temples.

She gave him a weak, quizzical look. "Yes, I am," she replied hoarsely. "Look, if you're a reporter, I can't talk now." She began to stand, shaking her head in embarrassment at being seen in such a state.

"No, I'm not a reporter. Please, may I sit with you for a moment?" he asked. She gave him a look of irritation for a second but was about to respond when he added, "I'm not a lawyer, either. Please. May I?" He asked in the same tone.

She turned her head to the side and nodded, feeling too weak to care, too exhausted to stand.

"What do you want?" she asked half-heartedly as she wiped her nose with the same ball of Kleenex. "Are you some sort of counselor or something? Listen, my husband and I don't have much money—"

"No, Mrs. Wallace. I'm not a counselor," he replied, cutting her off as he reached into his coat and brought out a clean white handkerchief. He handed it to her, and she looked at it for a moment with indecision. She took it and began dabbing at her nose and the forming tears in her eyes.

"Thank you," she said, trying to avoid the looks from other people coming up the courthouse steps, thankful that they did not recognize her.

He looked at her with the same compassionate gaze. "I am far from it. My wife is the counselor. She has a way of bonding with people. She was a mother, too."

The woman gave him a questioning look. "Was?" she asked, dabbing her cheeks. Seeing him closer, he now seemed familiar.

The man sat up straight, taking in a breath of the crisp early afternoon air before he replied. He had a confident look about him that she found attractive—a man with an aura of strength and security. She remembered Ron used to be like that. How could she be strong for both of them?

"My wife's name is Meredith. Meredith Richards."

The woman's eyes widened with realization. "Oh my God!" she exclaimed. "You're John! John Richards! I remember seeing you and your wife on those talk shows a while ago. I am so sorry!" She dabbed her eyes and face in a futile attempt to look presentable. Her eyes began to swell with more tears as she remembered. "Your daughter...and that bus driver who disappeared after the trial." She felt herself starting to break down again. The sobs caught in her throat quicker than she could contain them. "I am so... so..."

She didn't realize until moments later that she was crying on his shoulder as he held her, not saying a word as he comforted her with a shoulder rub as she wept. She kept thinking about the face of the Richards' daughter, how those eyes matched Davey's—eyes she would never see again...

She thought for a moment as he looked at her; his eyes conveyed more than any words could. Kind eyes. Strong eyes.

"How can I ever go on? My husband...how can we survive this?" she asked, her vision blurring again.

"We did, Mrs. Wallace. Someone showed us a way to... cope, you might say."

Recollection came to her. "And that theater that you and the other parents were involved in. The one where those orphan children performed for charity. I saw that on TV. The children's singing was beautiful. Raising all that money for... for the survivors of..."

Her lip trembled thinking about those children. She fought not to break down again as John smiled at her.

"We are all survivors in our own way, Mrs. Wallace. It may not seem like it now, but there is a way, and I can help you, along with a friend of mine."

She looked at him with a tinge of hopefulness. His words sounded so soothing. How could he sound so confident after all he and his wife had been through? Knowing that the man was freed and is still out there, somewhere. She couldn't imagine how they managed to overcome that and do these things for others...

"Please," she remarked, clearing her throat and trying to regain some composure, "please, call me Donna."

He smiled in a way that she could not identify. "Donna," he said, extending his hand for her to shake. As she took it, she felt how firm and warm his grip was. "Before you go inside, would you like to go somewhere for coffee? Nothing starts the healing process like a good cup of coffee," he remarked with a grin. "Or a bite to eat?"

ABOUT THE AUTHOR

Rick Powell is a resident of Oak Forest, Illinois, U.S.A. Rick began writing horror and dark fiction in 2012. His poetic and narrative talents have graced the pages of various publications, including Infernal Ink Magazine and the tantalizing anthology Lustcraftian Horrors: Erotic Stories Inspired by H.P. Lovecraft.

ABOUT THE PUBLISHER

Alas, who are we, marionettes on strings? And what do we stand for, puppeteers of our destiny?

I Ain't Your Marionette distinguishes itself as a stronghold of artistic liberation. At its helm, Marie Moldovan, once a marionette of circumstance, now orchestrates a symphony of narrative freedom. The company's sanctuary breathes life into marionette authors, whose tales of resilience and aspiration paint a vivid tableau of human spirit.

The press's hallmark anthologies, *Shattered Psyche* and *The Way of The Crow*, are more than mere collections; they are immersive experiences that beckon readers to venture beyond the mundane. Each story or visual masterpiece is a declaration of independence, a narrative that defies the norm and invites a reimagining of the world.

The *Voces Animarum* exhibition, alongside the *Shattered Psyche Traveling Showcase* and *Colours of Collaboration*, exemplifies the press's dedication to breaking new ground in literary and artistic expression. These ventures not only elevate the company's stature but also reverberate through the artistic community, transforming subdued creative murmurs into a powerful chorus that resonates far and wide.

Cut your strings and discover the creative freedom of **I Ain't Your Marionette Press** today at www.iaintyourmarionette.com.

FURTHER READING

Dive deeper into the captivating worlds crafted by Rick Powell. Each story in this collection explores the boundaries of love, loss, and the supernatural, inviting readers to confront their deepest fears and desires. Whether you're drawn to tales of obsession, apocalyptic nightmares, or chilling mysteries, there's something here for every lover of dark fiction.

Two Lost Souls:

Love, like life, is one of the oldest mysteries. But what happens when love turns into an obsession? When the boundaries between passion and madness blur, and the veil between the supernatural and natural world is cast aside? David believed his bond with his wife Helen was unbreakable, forged in the fires of life's trials. Yet, even the strongest love can be tested by the shadows that lurk in the corners of our hearts—and the darkness of a graveyard.

A Day of Ochre, Ascending:

In this apocalyptic nightmare inspired by Robert W. Chambers' The King in Yellow, a man's ordinary stroll with his dog turns into a nightmare. Each step plunges Walter and Archie deeper into a world of whispered doom. Will they escape, or will the nightmare consume them?

A Banquet of Panacea:

The loss of a child is a wound that never heals. But what if there was a way to move forward, a method so unthinkable it's only whispered about in the shadows? The Richards are living every parent's worst nightmare, their child's life stolen by a remorseless killer. In their darkest hour, they encounter Zhang, a billionaire with a chilling solution: when the justice system fails, he invites the families to a dinner shrouded in mystery and darkness.

Harold:

Frank is a seasoned detective with an uncanny 'feel' for things—a gift that has often guided him through the toughest cases. But this gift comes at a steep price. After years of risking his family and marriage for the job, Frank longs to slow down and reconnect with his loved ones. However, fate has other plans. A mysterious journal lands in his hands, chronicling the twisted crimes of a madman named Harold. Is this a work of fiction, or a chilling true-life account of a delusional killer?

Winston:

Julie lives with her mother in a rundown part of town, struggling to adjust to her mom's new boyfriend, a man she distrusts for many reasons. During a fateful walk home, she encounters Winston, an enigmatic old man whose presence is as captivating as it is mysterious. As their bond deepens, Julie's life begins to change in unimaginable ways. Who is Winston, and what secrets does he hold that

could lift Julie out of her adversity?
Is he a savior, or a messenger of
doom?

Ornament:

The holidays are a time for gathering
with friends, family, and loved ones.
Blazing fireplaces warm the bodies
and hearts of those closest to us, as
we share anecdotes of the year's
events while the snow and bitter cold
blow outside. But for Judith, the cold
seeps inside her home, reflecting the
turmoil in her life with John. Lies,
cheating, and psychological abuse
overshadow the season's joy, leaving
her without a solution in sight.

Messages:

In a world where technology races
forward, leaving yesterday's marvels
in the dust, what if someone dared to

blend ancient secrets with modern innovations? "Messages" delves into this terrifying possibility. Follow the harrowing journey of a reporter who uncovers the story of a lifetime—a story that could very well be his last. As he digs deeper, he finds himself trapped in a web of dark forces and apocalyptic realities.

A Glimpse Beyond the Veil:

The final book, *A Glimpse Beyond the Veil*, brings together all seven stories. Within this anthology of shadows, secrets writhe through the corridors of forgotten places and sinister whispers shroud the night. Each tale lures readers into the abyss to confront their deepest fears. This collection is a haunting exploration of the human condition and beckons readers to step into a world where reality blurs with the supernatural.

Thank you for your support.